MW00466240

The Walk

•

ROBERT WALSER

Translated by Christopher Middleton
with Susan Bernofsky

Introduction by Susan Bernofsky

A NEW DIRECTIONS PEARL

This edition of *The Walk* (*Der Spaziergang*) is a revision by Susan Bernofsky of Christopher Middleton's original translation.

Manufactured in the United States of America
New Directions Books are printed on acid-free paper
First published as a Pearl (NDP1231) by New Directions in 2012
Design by Erik Rieselbach

Library of Congress Cataloging-in-Publication Data
Walser, Robert, 1878–1956.
[Der Spaziergang. English]
The walk / Robert Walser.
p. cm.
"A New Directions Pearl."
ISBN 978-0-8112-1992-1 (acid-free paper)
I. Title.
PT2647.A64S613 2012
833'.912—dc23   2011049521

10 9 8 7 6 5 4

New Directions Books are published for James Laughlin
by New Directions Publishing Corporation
80 Eighth Avenue, New York 10011

Contents

THE WALK

Introduction

The book you hold in your hands is a quite peculiar case:
a revision of a translation that was perfectly splendid to
begin with. When the estimable Christopher Middleton
translated Robert Walser's iconic novella *The Walk* (Der
Spaziergang) in 1955, he didn't know that Walser himself
had subjected this story to a thorough revision, publishing the new version several years after the original edition, on which Middleton's translation was based. Read
side by side, the two versions are fascinating for the story
they tell about Walser's evolution as a writer. And so, to
give the English-language reader the opportunity to peer
over Walser's shoulder as he revises himself, I decided to
adjust Middleton's translation (with his blessing) to re-
flect the story's final version, making no changes other
than those dictated by Walser's own revisions. The result
is what you see here: Middleton's translation tweaked
by me, with words subtracted, rearranged, and in some
cases even added, so as to remain faithful both to Walser's

definite version of the story and to an English text I so greatly admire.

As far as I know, *The Walk* was the first of Walser's works to be translated into any language. In 1954, the young poet Christopher Middleton was teaching at the University of Zurich, and it was there thathe first encountered the work of the great Swiss modernist, thanks to his student Ernst Nef (himself a future writer): "I cannot remember if he showed me a book in the corridor outside the English seminar, or if he knocked at the window of my Zeltweg apartment and passed a book through the window when I opened it."[1]

Immersing himself in Walser's prose and combing antiquarian bookstores for first editions of his work, Middleton found Walser living "not only in his books and in the Herisau asylum, but everywhere in Zurich and in the bony faces of young peasants I saw in the train to Sankt Gallen one day. People on the streets, normal or eccentric, suddenly assumed identities, all of which, however variously, I measured against my image of Robert Walser or of his characters. I thought I could perceive a *spiritus helveticus* lurking under all the orthodoxy. As a maker of mischief, my Walser was enveloping everyone in a Walserian

1. Christopher Middleton, "Translation as a Species of Mime," in *The Review of Contemporary Fiction* 12:1 (1992), 50-56, 50.

aura. His prose was affecting me like Merlin in the Dark Ages, like Hermes in antiquity: my mind was projecting a spectacle in which all figures and events were essentially Walserian."[2]

Middleton never met Walser in person, even though Walser was still alive at the time, an elderly patient sequestered in the asylum at Herisau, where he would die on Christmas Day 1956 while out on a solitary walk, his work largely forgotten. But in the spring of 1955, Walser's guardian, Carl Seelig, told Walser of the young Englishman's translation, and he is said to have responded, "*So so,*" which translates as "My, my" or "Well, look at that." Seelig, Middleton recounts, rewarded his efforts with encouraging words and a snifter of cognac.

The Walk is an episodic comedy with darkness at the edges, its gravity becoming apparent only gradually as one follows the narrator's perambulations. The story marks a stylistic crossroads in Walser's work. He wrote it in Biel, the town of his birth, to which he had returned in 1913 after an absence of eighteen years. During that wartime period he retreated into a simpler narrative style than seen in his early work from Zurich and Berlin. Many of the stories he wrote in Biel seem straight-faced and earnest—the closest

2. Ibid.

Walser ever got to minimalism of any sort—compared to the thickly layered ironies of the Berlin period that preceded it. But the Biel years also saw the development of the mannered, manically repetitive style (in stories like "Nervous," "Knocking," "Fritz," and "Fräulein Knuchel") that later inspired Thomas Bernhard.[3] And the first published version of *The Walk* appears, to a lesser extent, imbued with that same manic energy, foregrounding the act of writing as part of the first-person narration. It was published as a slim stand-alone volume in 1917.

The second version appeared in Walser's 1920 collection *Seeland* (Lake Country). The revisions contained in it are at once massive and slight. "Slight" because he makes no changes at all to the story's structure or plot; "massive" because the changes he makes affect virtually every sentence as he tweaks and refines the prose. In many parts of the story (above all the opening and ending), he trims what he must have come to see as unnecessary verbiage, all those discursive adverbials and chattering asides that are often identified as quintessentially Walserian; at other points, though, he preserves them and in some cases even adds additional flourishes.

If Walser chose to tone down the first version's chatti-

3. The first two appear in *Selected Stories of Robert Walser* (New York Review Books Classics), the others in *Masquerade and Other Stories* (Johns Hopkins University Press).

ness at certain key points, I believe it was for the sake of minimizing the divide between the writing protagonist and the walking protagonist. As in many of his works (notably the novel *The Robber*) these are one and the same person; but in the first version of *The Walk* there is a greater discrepancy of mood between them, and the writing narrator's nattering on about the writing process diverts attention from the walker's subtly shifting frame of mind. While this walker displays an almost blithe playfulness toward the people and institutions he encounters, it gradually becomes clear that there is something he is desperately trying to banish from his thoughts. It is this desperation that drives him to tear through the city on one distracting errand after the other, the actual goal of these errands being distraction itself.

Not that the tone of the story becomes exactly solemn in the revised version. The chirp becomes a chirplet, but it still can be heard. Most of Walser's changes are subtle. He trims verbiage everywhere (e.g., "At this I felt moved to say" becomes "At this I said"). He adds paragraph breaks and rearranges the order of many of the short lists of nouns, verbs, and adjectives found throughout the story. Often this reordering is clearly intended to heighten the comedy of a passage, such as when the narrator in the first version announces that he is planning to "eat, carouse, and dine in the palazzo, or house, of Frau Aebi"; the revision has him instead descending bathetically from the elegant "dine" to the humble "eat."

The parts of the story that change most in revision are the opening and conclusion. Walser rewrites the final passage to define the narrator's relationship with his lost beloved more explicitly, and the story's opening lines are streamlined, launching the action with far less meta-commentary.

In Middleton's original translation, the opening reads:

> I have to report that one fine morning, I do not know any more for sure what time it was, as the desire to take a walk came over me, I put my hat on my head, left my writing room, or room of phantoms, and ran down the stairs to hurry out into the street. I might add that on the stairs I encountered a woman who looked like a Spaniard, a Peruvian, or a Creole. She presented to the eye a certain pallid, faded majesty. But I must strictly forbid myself a delay of even two seconds with this Brazilian lady, or whatever she might be; for I may waste neither space nor time. As far as I can remember as I write this down, I found myself, as I walked into the open, bright, and cheerful street, in a romantically adventurous state of mind, which pleased me profoundly.

In the revised version:

> One morning, as the desire to take a walk came over me, I put my hat on my head, left my writing room, or room of phan-

toms, and ran down the stairs to hurry out into the street. On the stairs I encountered a woman who looked like a Spaniard, a Peruvian, or a Creole and presented to the eye a certain pallid, faded majesty.

As far as I remember, I found myself, as I walked into the open, bright, and cheerful street, in a romantically adventurous state of mind, which pleased me.

Walser excises most of the references to the act of composition ("I have to report," "I might add," and so on), but he does preserve one of them ("As far as I remember"), which suffices to establish the present tense of narration.

While Walser makes adjustments to nearly every sentence in his revision, most of these changes—particularly in the middle of the story—are subtle, slight adjustments to diction and word order, and will not appear particularly striking to those familiar with Middleton's translation. Most of my changes are simply a matter of rearranging the elements of a sentence, or replacing an isolated word or phrase. Sometimes the translation of a subsequently revised passage is left to stand because, with uncanny frequency, Middleton's translation actually anticipates Walser's own changes. For example, when Walser has a boastful chef proclaim, "Tatsächlich gehen aus unserer exquisiten Küche Meisterwerke der Kochkunst hervor," Middleton's translates, "From our exquisite cuisine proceed veritable masterpieces of culinary art." The word "veritable" does not correspond to anything in the German; Middleton added it for rhythm and tone, as a translator is certainly entitled. But Walser's own revision follows suit, turning these masterpieces into "wahre Meisterwerke" (true or veritable masterpieces). Eerily, Middleton sometimes also trims the same bits Walser later excises. The sentence "You have perhaps before today never been so unceremoniously addressed" omits the closing phrase "noch von keinem Menschen hier" ("by any person here"), which Walser, too, later cuts. Both Walser and Middleton even correct the same mixed metaphor: "The pines stood straight as pillars there" omits the adverb originally included: *kerzengerade* (*candle*-straight).

In editing Middleton's translation, I have taken pains not to make any changes that do not respond directly to changes made by Walser himself, except in a few cases regarding punctuation where I felt that the addition of a dash or a semicolon would improve legibility and comprehension.

Reading and rereading Middleton's translation of the 1917 *Walk* while preparing this revised edition, I was struck again and again by how beautifully his English captures the essence of the Walserian spirit, that mix of solemnity and whimsy, impertinence and veneration that comprise Walser's voice. Revising—adding to, subtracting from, and rearranging the phrases of Middleton's original rendering of the first version of Walser's story to arrive at a translation of Walser's 1920 revision—has only increased my admiration. I am grateful to him for giving his blessing to this enterprise and for allowing me to add my translator's voice to his.

I am also grateful to my fellow Walser scholar Fuminari Niimoto for suggesting this project, to Ian Solheim for technical support, and to my editors Barbara Epler and Michael Barron, who provided invaluable help in the preparation of this edition.

— SUSAN BERNOFSKY

The Walk

ONE MORNING, as the desire to take a walk came over me, I put my hat on my head, left my writing room, or room of phantoms, and ran down the stairs to hurry out into the street. On the stairs I encountered a woman who looked like a Spaniard, a Peruvian, or a Creole, and presented to the eye a certain pallid, faded majesty.

As far as I remember, I found myself, as I walked into the open, bright, and cheerful street, in a romantically adventurous state of mind, which pleased me. The morning world spread out before my eyes appeared as beautiful to me as if I saw it for the first time. Everything I saw made upon me a delightful impression of friendliness, of goodliness, and of youth. I quickly forgot that up in my room I had only just a moment before been brooding gloomily over a blank sheet of paper. Sorrow, pain, and grave thoughts were as vanished, although I vividly sensed a certain seriousness still before me and behind me.

I was tense with eager expectation of whatever might

encounter me or cross my way on my walk. My steps were measured and calm. As I went on my way, I presented, as far as I know, a fairly dignified appearance. My feelings I like to conceal from the eyes of my fellow men, of course without any fearful strain to do so—such strain I would consider a great error.

I had not yet gone twenty or thirty steps over a broad and crowded square, when Professor Meili, a foremost authority, brushed by me.

Incontrovertible power in person, serious, ceremonial, and majestical, Professor Meili trod his way; in his hand he held an unbendable scientific walking stick, which infused me with dread, reverence, and esteem. Meili's nose was a sharp, imperative, stern hawk- or eagle-nose. His mouth was juridically clamped tight and squeezed shut. The famous scholar's gait was like an iron law. From Professor Meili's adamant eyes, world history and the afterglow of long-gone heroic deeds flashed out. His hat was like an irremovable ruler. Secret rulers are the most proud and most implacable. Yet, on the whole, Professor Meili carried himself with a tenderness, as if he needed in no way whatsoever to make apparent what quantities of power and gravity he personified. Since I permitted myself the thought that men who do not smile in a sweet and beautiful way can nonetheless be honorable and trustworthy, he appeared sympathetic to me in spite of his severity. As is well known, there are people who excel at concealing the crimes which they commit behind disarming, obliging behavior.

I catch a glimpse of a bookseller along with a book shop; likewise soon, as I guess and observe, a bakery with gold lettering comes in for a mention. But first I have a parson to record. With a kind face, a bicycling town chemist cycles close by the walker; similarly, a regimental or staff doctor. An unassuming pedestrian should not remain unrecorded, namely a bric-a-brac vendor and rag collector who has become rich. It should be noted that young boys and girls, free and unrestrained, race around in the sunlight.

"Let them be unrestrained as they are, for age, alas, will one day, soon enough, terrify and bridle them," I mused.

In the water of a fountain a dog refreshes itself, in the blue air swallows twitter. One or two ladies in astonishingly short skirts and astoundingly high, snug, fine, elegant, dainty colored bootees make themselves as conspicuous as anything else. Moreover two summer or straw hats catch my eye. The story about the straw hats is this: it is that in the bright, gentle air I suddenly see two enchanting hats; under the hats stand two fairly prosperous-looking gentlemen, who by means of a bold, elegant, courteous waving of hats seem to be bidding each other good morning, which is an occasion upon which the hats

are evidently more important than their wearers and own-
ers. The writer is nonetheless very humbly asked to be a bit
careful to avoid jokes as well as other superfluousnesses. It
is hoped that he understands this, once and for all.

As now a splendid bookshop came most pleasantly to
my notice, and I felt the desire to bestow upon it a fleeting
visit, I did not hesitate to step in, with the best of grace,
while I admittedly thought that in me might possibly appear more a rigorous bookkeeper, or inspector, a collector
of news items, or a sensitive connoisseur, than a welcome,
favorite, wealthy book buyer or good client.

In courteous, exceedingly circumspect tones, I inquired,
choosing understandably only the finest turns of speech,
after the latest and best in the field of belles-lettres.

"May I," I asked with diffidence, "take a moment to ac-
quaint myself with, and taste the fine qualities of, the most
sterling and serious, and therefore of course the most read
and most quickly acknowledged and purchased, reading
matter? You would pledge me to unusual gratitude were
you to be so kind as to lay generously before me that book
which, as certainly nobody can know so precisely as you,
has found the highest place in the estimation of the reading public, as well as that of the dreaded and thence surely
flatteringly circumvented critics, and which furthermore
has made them merry.

"Indeed I am uncommonly keen to be permitted to

learn which of all the works of the pen piled high or put on show here is the favorite book in question, the sight of which will quite probably make me at once a joyous and enthusiastic purchaser. My longing to see the preferred author of the cultivated world and his universally admired, thunderously applauded masterpiece before me, and, as I said, probably also to be able to buy the same, ripples through all my limbs.

"Might I most politely, and as urgently as possible, ask you to show me such a most successful book, so that this desire which has seized me might acknowledge itself gratified, and cease to trouble me?"

"Certainly," said the bookseller.

Like an arrow he vanished out of eyeshot, to return already the next instant—bearing indeed the most bought and read book of real enduring value in his hand—to his anxious potential client.

This delicious fruit of the spirit he carried carefully and solemnly, as if carrying a relic charged with sanctifying magic. His face was enraptured; his manner radiated the deepest awe. With that smile on his lips which one finds only with those who are inspirited to the deepest core, he laid before me in the most winning way that which he had brought. I considered the book, and asked:

"Could you swear that this is the most widely distributed book of the year?"

"Without a doubt!"

"Could you insist that this is the book which one absolutely has to have read?"

"Unconditionally."

"Is this book definitely good?"

"An utterly superfluous and completely inadmissible
question!"

"In that case, thank you most kindly," said I cold-blood-
edly, left the book—which had been without question
most widely distributed because everyone had unconditionally to read it—as I chose, where it was, and withdrew
without further ceremony, i.e. as softly as could be.

"Uncultivated, ignorant man!" shouted the bookseller
after me, for he was most justifiably vexed. But, letting
him have his say, I walked at my ease on my way, which,
to be accurate, as I shall at once expound and discuss at
length, led into the next stately banking establishment.

The very place I wished to inquire at and receive reli-
able information about certain securities. "To hop into
a money institute, just in passing," I said to myself, "in
order to manage one's financial affairs, and to produce
questions, which one utters in no more than a whisper, is
pleasant, and looks, no doubt, exceedingly good."

"It is good and wonderfully convenient that you come
to us in person," the official responsibly countering at
the counter said to me, in a friendly tone. With an almost

knavish, at any rate very charming smile, he proceeded as follows:

"Only today, you see, we were about to communicate to you in writing what will now be communicated to you orally, namely something which will be for you without a doubt a gladdening piece of information, that we are instructed by a society, or circle, of what are evidently well-disposed, good-natured, philanthropic ladies, not so much to place to your debit as instead, and this will of course be fundamentally more welcome to you, to credit your account with

One Thousand Francs

a transaction of which you will be so kind as to take, at once, mental or any other form of note which may suit you. This information will surely please you; for upon us you make, we must confess, an impression such as tells us—as we would like to permit ourselves to say—with almost all too excessive clarity, that you very definitely need alleviation of a delicate nature.

"The money is at your disposal with effect from today.

"Your features are suffused this very moment with an appreciably great joy. Your eyes are shining. Your mouth, perhaps for the first time in years, because pressing daily troubles (and consequently a sorrowful mood and all sorts of dark thoughts) have forbidden you laughter, now has about it unmistakably a trace of laughter. Your previously darkened brow looks decidedly serene.

"In any case you can rub your hands and be glad that some noble and kind benefactresses, moved by the sublime thought that to allay a man's distress is beautiful, and to dam up his grief is good, wished to see a poor, unsuccessful poet receive assistance.

"On the fact that persons were found whose desire was to condescend to remember you, and additionally on this occasion of evidence that fortunately there are individuals who cannot regard with indifference the existence of a poet apparently often despised, we congratulate you."

"The sum of money so unexpectedly bestowed upon me by such indulgent ladies' or—as I might almost have said—fairies' hands," I said, "I shall leave without more ado in your charge, where it will certainly be best preserved, since you have at your disposal fireproof and thief-tight safes, in which treasures seem to be carefully kept from destruction of any sort, or from any abolition whatsoever. Besides, you pay interest, do you not? May I, by the way, politely ask for a receipt?

"To withdraw, at any time according to my need, from the large sum small sums is a liberty I assume I shall be accorded.

"Since I am thrifty, I shall know how to manage the gift like a methodical, steady man. I shall have, in a polite, considerate letter, to express the necessary gratitude to my kind donators, which I think I shall take care of tomorrow morning, so that it does not get forgotten through procrastination.

"Your assumption, which you just now voiced so frankly, albeit cautiously, that I might be poor, could rest upon a basis of accurate and quite acute observation. But that I know what I know, and that I myself am well informed about my own modest person at all times, suffices entirely. Appearances frequently deceive, and delivering a judgment upon some man is something the man himself will best accomplish, for surely no one can know a person who has experienced all sorts of things better than he does himself.

"Often I wandered, to be sure, perplexed in a mist and in a thousand dilemmas, seeing myself vacillating and often wretchedly forsaken. Yet I believe that struggling for life can only be a fine thing. It is not with pleasures and with joys that an honest man might grow proud. Rather in the roots of his soul it can only be through trial bravely undergone, deprivation patiently endured, that he becomes proud and gay. On this point, however, one does not like to waste words.

"Where did there live a man who was never in his life without sustenance? What human being has ever seen as the years pass his hopes, plans, and dreams completely undestroyed? When was there ever a soul that never had to deduct a discount from the sum total of its bold long-ings, its lofty, sweet imaginings of happiness?"

Receipt for one thousand francs was handed out, or in, to our steady creditor and accounted competitor, whereupon he was entitled to bid good day as well as to withdraw.

My heart glad that this capital sum should come flying to me, magically, as from a blue sky, I ran out of the high vestibule into the open air, to go on walking.

Since nothing new and shrewd wants to strike me at the moment, I hope I may add that I carried in my pocket an invitation card from Frau Aebi that most humbly re-quested me to be so good as to appear punctually at half past twelve at Frau Aebi's home for a modest lunch. I quite firmly intended to obey the estimable summons and to emerge promptly at the time stated in the presence of the person in question.

Since, dear reader, you give yourself the trouble to march along with the inventor and writer of these lines attentively out forthwith into the bright and good morn-ing air, not hurrying and hastily, but rather quite tidily, at ease, with level head, discreetly, smoothly, and calmly, now we both arrive in front of the aforementioned bakery with the boastful gold inscription, where we stop, horri-fied, because we feel inclined to be exceedingly dismayed as well as honestly astonished at the gross ostentation and at the disfigurement of the sweetest rusticity which is intimately connected with it.

Spontaneously I exclaimed: "Pretty indignant, by God, should one be, when brought face to face with such golden inscriptional barbarities, which impress upon our rustic surrounds the seal of greed, moneygrubbing, and a miserable coarsening of the soul. Does a master baker really require to appear so huge, with his foolish proclamations, to beam forth and glitter, like a dressy, dubious lady? Let him bake and knead his bread in honest, reasonable modesty. What sort of vertiginous conditions are we beginning to live in, when the municipality, the neighbors, officials, and public opinion not only tolerate but unhappily, it is clear, even applaud that which injures every sense of good office, every sense of beauty and probity, that which is morbidly puffed up, thinks it must offer a ridiculous, miserable, tawdry show of itself screaming out over a hundred yards' distance into the good air: 'Such and such am I. I have so and so much money, and I dare to make an unpleasant impression. Of course I am a bumpkin, a blockhead with my hideous ostentation, a taste-deficient fellow. But there will scarcely be anyone to forbid me to be blockheaded.'

"Do far-gleaming, loathsomely boastful golden letters stand in any acceptable, honorably justified relation or in any healthy affinitive proportion to … bread? Not in the least.

"But loathsome boasting and swaggering began somewhere or other, and like a lamentable flood advanced step by step, bearing foolishness and garbage along with them.

They have affected also my respectable baker, spoiled his earlier good taste, and undermined his inborn decency. I would probably give my left leg, or left arm, if by such a sacrifice I could help recall the fine old sense of sincerity, the old, good, noble sufficiency, and restore to country and to people the modesty and respectability which, to the sorrow of all men who seek honesty, have been plentifully lost.

"Every miserable desire to seem more than one is should go to the devil, for this is a veritable catastrophe. This and similar things spread danger of war, death, misery, hate, and vilification over the earth, and puts upon all that exists an abominable mask of malice and abhorrent egoism. I would not have a simple workman a lord, nor a simple woman her ladyship. But everything nowadays is out to dazzle, to be glitteringly new and exquisite and beautiful and noble and exceedingly elegant, to be lord and lady, it's practically scandalous. But a time will perhaps come again when things will be different. I would like to hope so."

On account of this haughty bearing, this domineering attitude, I shall soon, as will be learned, have to take myself to task. In what manner will also soon be shown. It would not be good if I were to criticize others mercilessly, yet treat myself as tenderly and indulgently as possible. As I see it, abuses of writing should not be practiced—a sentence that ought to please all and sundry, meet with warm applause, and inspire vigorous satisfaction.

Left of the country road here, a foundry full of work-men causes a noticeable disturbance. In recognition of this I am honestly ashamed to be merely out for a walk like this while many others drudge and labor. Though to be sure, I myself perhaps drudge away at times, when all these industrious workmen have knocked off themselves and are taking a rest.

In passing, a fitter calls to me: "It looks to me you're out for a walk again, working hours too!" I laugh and wave to him and blithely admit that he is right.

Without the least annoyance at having been found out, for that would have been silly, I walked merrily on.

In my bright yellow English suit, which I had received as a present, I really seemed to myself, as I frankly admit, something like a lord and grand seigneur, a marquis strolling up and down his park, although the place I walked was only a semi-rural, semi-suburban, neat, modest, nice little poor-quarter and country road, and on no account a park, as I was just now so arrogant as to suppose, a presumption I gently withdraw, because all that is parklike is mere invention and does not fit here at all.

Factories both great and small and mechanical work-shops lay scattered agreeably in green countryside. Fat cozy farms meanwhile kindly offered their arms to hammering, knocking industry, which always has something skinny and worn-out about it. Nut, cherry, and plum trees gave the soft rounded road an attractive, entertaining, and delicate character.

Across the middle of the road, which I found as a matter of fact quite beautiful and loved, lay a dog. In fact almost everything I saw as I proceeded filled me with a fiery love. A second pretty dog scene was as follows:

A large yet comical, harmless, humorous fellow of a dog was quietly staring at a wee scrap of a boy who crouched on some porch steps and, on account of the attention which the assuredly good-natured yet nonetheless somewhat terrifying-looking animal chose to pay him, set up a childish, fearful wail. I found the scene enchanting. A further childish scene in this little quotidian or country road theater I found even more delightful and enchanting.

On the rather dusty road two small children were lying, as in a garden. One child said to the other: "Now give me a nice little kiss." The other child obeyed. Hereupon said the first: "All right, now you may get up." Without a sweet little kiss he would probably never have allowed the other what he now permitted it.

"How well this naïve scene goes with the blue sky, which laughs down with such divine beauty upon the bright, gay earth," I exclaimed and gave the following brief but earnest speech:

"Children are heavenly because they are always in a kind of heaven. When they grow older, their heaven vanishes. Then they fall out of their childishness into the dry, tedious, calculating manner and the utilitarian, highly respectable perceptions of adults. For the children of poor folk the country road in summer is like a play-room. Where else can they go, seeing that the gardens are selfishly closed to them? Woe to the automobiles driving by, as they ride coldly and maliciously into the children's games, into the child's heaven, putting small, innocent human beings in danger of being crushed to a pulp. The terrible thought that a child actually can be run over by such a clumsy triumphal car, I thrust it aside, otherwise my wrath will seduce me to coarse expressions, with which it is well known nothing much ever gets done."

To people sitting in a blustering automobile I always present an austere face. Then they believe that I am a sharp-eyed, malevolent spy, a plainclothes policeman, delegated by high officials to spy on the traffic, to note down the numbers of vehicles, and later to report them to the proper authorities. I always then look darkly at the wheels, at the car as a whole, but never at its occupants, whom I despise, and this in no way personally, but purely on principle, for I never shall understand, how it can be called a pleasure to hurtle past all the images and objects which our beautiful earth displays, as if one had gone mad and had to accelerate for fear of despair.

In fact, I love all repose and all that reposes, all thrift and moderation, and am in my inmost self, unfriendly toward any haste and agitation. More than what in God's name is true I need not say, and because of the words I've just uttered, this irksome zooming of automobiles and their evil air-polluting smell, which nobody can possibly love or esteem, will certainly not be discontinued once and for all. As for the fragrance in question, it would be unnatural if someone's nostrils were to inhale it with relish, which however can scarcely ever have been the case. Enough, and no harm meant, and now walk on. Oh, it is delightful, and in goodness and simplicity most ancient, to walk on foot, provided of course one's shoes or boots are in order.

Would the esteemed ladies and gentlemen, patrons and patronesses and circles of readers, while they benevolently tolerate and condone so solemn, high-strutting a style, now be so kind as to allow me duly to draw their attention to two particularly significant figures, persons, or forms, namely firstly, or better, first, to an alleged retired actress, and secondly to the most youthful presumed budding cantatrice?

I hold these two people to be considerably weighty and therefore I believed it wise to announce them properly in advance, before they enter and figure in reality, so that an odor of significance and fame may run before these two gentle creatures, and they may be received and observed on their appearance with all distinction, due regard, and loving concern, such as one should, in my diminutive opinion, almost compulsorily accord to such beings.

Then at about half past twelve the writer will, as is known, in reward for surviving these labors, carouse, dine, and eat in the palazzo, or house, of Frau Aebi. Till then, however, he will have to cover considerable stretches of his road, as well as writing a fair quantity of lines. But one realizes to be sure to satiety that he loves to walk as well as he loves to write; the latter of course perhaps just a shade less than the former.

In front of a very attractive house, a woman sat on a bench very close to the road, and hardly had I glimpsed her when I plucked up the courage to speak, addressing her, in the most polite terms possible, as follows:

"Forgive me, a person utterly unknown to you, to whose lips the eager and assuredly saucy question forces itself at the sight of you, whether you have not been formerly an actress. For in fact you seem very much indeed like a once great, celebrated stage artist. Certainly you quite rightly wonder at my so amazingly rash and obstreperous address. But you have such a beautiful face, such a pleasant and—as I would like to add—interesting appearance, present such a fine aspect, look so candidly, majestically, calmly out of your eyes upon me as upon the world in general, that I could not possibly have compelled myself to pass you by without daring to say something or other flattering to you, which I hope you will not hold against me, although I am afraid that I deserve, if not correction, at least admonishment on account of my frivolity.

"When I saw you, it at once occurred to me that you must have been an actress, and today you sit here beside the simple road, in front of this small, appealing shop, whose owner you appear to me to be.

"Probably you have before today never been so unceremoniously addressed. Your graceful aspect, your beautiful appearance, your hospitable equanimity, and this fine, noble, cheerful figure in your advancing years encourage me to engage with you in conversation on the open road. This fine day also, delighting me as it does with its freedom and gaiety, has kindled in me a joyousness, in consequence of which I have perhaps gone too far with an unknown lady.

"You smile! Then you are in no way angered by the unconstrained quality of my utterance. I think it splendid when from time to time two persons who are otherwise unacquainted freely and intimately converse, for which converse we inhabitants of this wandering planet—which is a puzzle to us—do, when all is said and done, possess mouth and tongue and linguistic capacity, which last is as a matter of fact singularly lovely.

"In any case I liked you profoundly straightaway. Could such an unguarded confession cause you to be angry with me?"

"It is far rather a pleasure for me," said the beautiful woman happily; "but, in reference to your supposition, I must prepare you for a disappointment. I have never been an actress."

At this I said: "Not long ago I came here out of cold, disadvantageous circumstances, without any sort of confidence, without faith, inwardly sick, utterly without hope. I was hostile to the world and to myself, and a stranger to both. Mistrust and timidity accompanied my every step. Then, little by little, I lost my sorrowful, ignoble prejudices that sprang from all manner of oppression and breathed again more unconstrainedly, quiet and free, and gradually became again a warmer, better, and happier man. I saw many terrors gradually vanish; absence of hope and all the uncertainty I'd had to carry about with me were slowly transformed into gay content and lively, pleasant sympathy, which I learned to feel anew. I was as if dead; but now it is as if I were being raised up and set on my way, or as if I had just arisen from the grave and returned to life. Where I thought I must meet with much that is repulsive, disquieting, hard, I encounter charm and goodness, I find all imaginable docility, comfort, edification and goodness."

"So much the better," said the woman, and her face and voice were kind.

As the moment seemed to have come to conclude this

conversation, somewhat truculently begun, and to with-draw, I presented my compliments to the woman with, I should add, an exquisite and very scrupulous courtesy, bowed to her respectfully and, as if nothing in the least had transpired, walked quietly on my way.

A modest question: An elegant milliner's under the green of the trees, might this perhaps by now arouse exceptional interest and evoke possibly a little if any applause?

Seeing as I firmly believe it does, I dare to observe that as I walked and marched along on the most beautiful of roads a juvenile, foolish shout of joy burst from my throat, a throat which scarcely considered this, or anything like it, possible.

What did I see and discover that was new and astounding? Oh, quite simply the above-mentioned milliner's and fashion salon.

Paris and St. Petersburg, Bucharest and Milan, London and Berlin—all that is elegant, naughty, and metropolitan—drew close to me, emerged before me, to dazzle, beguile, fascinate me. But in the capitals of the world one misses the green and luscious embellishments of trees, the beneficence and magic of friendly fields, the ornamentation of many darling leaves and, last but not least, the fragrance of flowers, and all of this I had here.

"All this," so I proposed resolutely, "I shall soon sketch and write down in a piece or sort of fantasy, which I shall entitle 'The Walk.' Especially this ladies' hat shop may not be omitted, as otherwise, a truly significant charm would be missing from the piece."

Feathers, ribbons, artificial flowers and fruits on the nice quaint hats were to me almost as attractive as comely nature herself, who, with her green and other warm colors, delightfully framed the artificial colors and fantastic shapes, such that the milliner's might have been simply a charming painting. I rely here on the most subtle readerly understanding. I am honestly and constantly afraid of readers of all sorts. This miserable and cowardly confession is, in my estimation, all too understandable. It is the same with all the more courageous authors.

God! what did I see, likewise under leaves, but a bewitching, dainty butcher shop, with rose-red pork, beef, and lamb displayed. The butcher was bustling about inside, where his customers stood also. Is not this butcher shop at least as well worth a shout as the shop with the hats?

A grocer's might merit a quiet mention.

To all sorts of public houses I shall come later, which is, I think, quite soon enough. With public houses, doubtless one cannot begin late enough in the day, because they produce consequences which everybody knows to satiety. The most virtuous person does not dispute the fact that he is never master of certain improprieties. Be that as it may, one is of course—human, luckily, and as such fabulously easy to pardon, since every one of us can quite simply appeal to the weak system he was born with.

Here once again I must take fresh bearings.

I am surely justified in assuming that I can effect the reorganization and regrouping of forces as well as any field marshal surveying all circumstances and drawing all contingencies and reverses into the net of his, I am permitted to say, genius for computation.

An industrious person at present can read things of this sort daily in the daily papers. Assuredly he notes such choice expressions as "flank attack," etc.

Might I confess that I have recently come to the conclusion that the art of war can be just as difficult, and require almost as much patience, as the art of writing, the converse being also true?

Writers also, much like generals, often make the most laborious preparations before they dare march to the attack and give battle: in other words, fling their book or artistic or shoddy product into the book market, an action which sometimes vigorously provokes very forceful counterattacks. As is known, books attract potentially relevant discussions, which sometimes end in such a fury that the book must disappear at once, while apparently the lamentable, poor, miserable writer pitiably asphyxiates and quite doubtless despairs of it all.

I hope no estrangement will ensue if I say that I am writing all these I trust pretty sentences, letters, and lines with a quill from the Imperial High Court of Justice. Hence my brevity, pregnancy, and acumen, possibly at certain points well enough perceptible, at which nobody need wonder any more.

But when shall I come at last to the well-earned banquet with my Frau Aebi? As I fear, it will take quite a time, as sundry and considerable obstacles must first be put aside. I've had an unstintedly abundant appetite long enough.

As I went on my way, like a better sort of tramp, a vagabond, pickpocket, idler or vagrant of a sort finer than some, past all sorts of contented gardens planted full with placid vegetables, past flowers and fragrance of flowers, past fruit trees and past bean shrubs full of beans, past towering, delightful crops, as rye, barley, and wheat, past a wood-yard containing wood and wood shavings, past juicy grass and a gently splashing little waterway, rivulet, or stream, past all sorts of people, as choice trade-plying market women tripping gently past, and past a festive clubhouse decoratively hung with banners flying for joy, and also past many other good-hearted, useful things, past a particularly beautiful little fairy apple tree, and past God knows what else in the way of feasible things, for example strawberry blossoms or, even better, gracefully past the ripe, red strawberries, while all sorts of thoughts continued to preoccupy me, since, when I'm out walking,

many notions, flashes of light, and lightning flashes quite
of their own accord intrude and interrupt, to be carefully
pondered upon, there came a man in my direction, an
enormity and monster, who almost completely darkened
my bright road, a lanky beanpole of a fellow, sinister,
whom I knew only too well, a very curious customer;
namely the giant Tomzack.

In any other place, on any other road but this dear,
yielding country road I would have expected him. His
sorrowful, gruesome air infused me with terror, and his
tragic, atrocious appearance took every bright, beautiful
prospect, all joy and gaiety away from me on the spot.

Tomzack! It is true, dear reader, is it not, the name alone
has the sound of terrible, mournful things? "Why do you
persecute me, why need you meet me here in the middle of
the road?" I cried to him. But Tomzack gave me no answer.

He turned his great eyes upon me, that is, looked down
from high up on me below. He surpassed me in length and
height by very considerable degrees; beside him, I felt like
a dwarf, or like a poor, weak little child. With the greatest
of ease the giant could have crushed me or trodden me
underfoot.

Oh, I knew who he was. For him there was no rest.
He slept in no soft bed, lived in no comfortable, homely
house. He was at home everywhere and nowhere. He had
no home country, and so was nowhere a citizen. Completely without happiness he lived, without love, without

motherland and human joy.

He had sympathy with no man, and so with him and his mopping and mowing no man had sympathy. Past, present, and future were to him an insubstantial desert, and life appeared to be too small, too narrow for him. For him nothing existed which had meaning; and he himself in turn meant something to nobody at all. Out of his eyes there broke a glare of grief from underworlds and overworlds, and indescribable pain spoke from each of his slack and weary movements.

Not dead, but also not alive, neither old nor young was he. A hundred thousand years old he seemed to me, and it furthermore seemed to me that he must live for eternity, only to be for eternity no living being. Every instant he was dying and yet he could not die. For him there was nowhere a grave with flowers on it. Eluding him, I murmured to myself: "Goodbye, keep well nevertheless, friend Tomzack!"

Without looking back at the phantom, pitiful superman, unfortunate specter—and candidly I could not have the remotest desire to do so—I walked on and soon afterwards, proceeding thus in warm, yielding air and erasing the sad impression which the strange figure of a giant had made upon me, I came into a pine forest, through which coiled a smiling, serpentine, and at the same time roguishly graceful path, which I followed with pleasure.

Path and forest floor were as a carpet. Here within the

forest it was quiet as in a happy human soul, as in a temple or enchanted castle and dream-wrapped fairy-tale palace, as in Sleeping Beauty's castle, where all sleep, and all are hushed for centuries of long years. I penetrated deeper, and I speak perhaps a little indulgently if I say that to myself I seemed like a prince with golden hair clad in warrior's armor.

So solemn was it in the forest that dulcet imaginings, as if of their own accord, took possession of the sensitive walker there. How glad this sweet forest softness and repose made me!

From time to time, from outside, a slight sound or two penetrated the seclusion and bewitching sweet darkness, perhaps a bang, a whistle, or some other noise, whose distant note would only intensify the prevailing soundlessness, which I inhaled to my very heart's content, and whose virtues I drank and quaffed with due ceremony.

In all this tranquility a bird here and there let his blithe voice be heard out of a charmed, holy hiding place. I stood and listened. Suddenly there came upon me an unnameable feeling for the world, and, together with it, a feeling of gratitude, which broke powerfully out of my joyful soul. The pines stood straight as pillars there, and not the least thing moved in the whole delicate forest, throughout which all kinds of inaudible voices seemed to sound and echo and all sorts of visible-invisible figures roamed.

Music out of the primeval world, from whence I cannot tell, stole on my ear.

"Thus, if it must be, shall I then willingly die. A memory will then enliven me even in death and a joy delight me even in the grave, a thanksgiving for the pleasures and an ecstatic giving-thanks."

High up, a gentle rustling from the treetops could be heard. "To love and to kiss here must be divinely beautiful," I told myself. Simply to tread on the ground became a pleasure. The stillness kindled prayers in the feeling soul. "To lie here inconspicuous in the cool forest earth must be sweet. That one might still sense and enjoy death even in death! To have a grave in the forest would be lovely. Perhaps I should hear the birds singing and the rustling above me. I would like such a thing as that." Marvelous between trunks of oaks a pillar of sunbeams fell into the forest, which to me seemed like a green, delicious grave. Soon, however, I stepped out into life again, into the radiant open.

Now there should come to the fore, as it emerges here, an attractive, fine inn with a charming garden full of refreshing shade. The garden should lie on a pretty hill with a good view all around; right beside it there should stand or lie an extra, artificial hill, or bastion, where one could stay for quite a long time to enjoy the splendid prospect. A glass of beer or wine would also certainly not be unwelcome. The person who is out walking here, however, recalls just in time that his excursion is by no means strenuous. The toilsome mountains lie far off in the bluish, white-misted distance. He frankly confesses that his thirst is neither murderous nor heathenish, since till now he has had to cover only relatively short stretches of the road. Indeed, it is here a question more of a delicate, prudent walk than of an excursion or voyage, more a subtle circular stroll than a forced ride and march. Therefore he justly, as well as wisely, declines to enter the house of joy and refreshment, and he takes his leave.

All serious people who read this will certainly accord him affluent applause for his fine decision and goodwill. Did I not, as much as an hour ago, take the opportunity of announcing a young songstress? Now she enters.

Enters, that is, at a ground-level window.

For when I returned from the forest recess to the highway now, I heard—but stop! Relax in brief respite.

Writers who understand their profession at least a little take the same as easily as possible. From time to time they like to lay their pens aside a while. Uninterrupted writing fatigues, like digging.

What I heard from the ground-level window was the most delicious, fresh folk or opera song, a matutinal banquet of sound, a morning concert, which entered my astonished ears completely free of charge.

At her drab suburban window, a young girl was standing in her bright dress, still a schoolgirl, but slim already and tall, singing out and up into the bright air simply ecstatically.

Most agreeably surprised, and enchanted by the unexpected song, I stood a little to the side so as to neither disturb the singer nor rob myself of my attendance and concomitant pleasure.

The song which the little one sang seemed to be of an utterly cheerful, joyful nature. The notes had the very sound itself of young innocent joy in life and in love; they flew, like angel figures wearing the snow-white plumage of delight, up into the blue heavens, whence they seemed to fall down again in order to die smiling. It was like dying from affliction, dying perhaps from too great a delight, like a too exultant loving and living, a powerlessness to live any more—the vision of life was too rich, too beautiful and delicate, such that to some extent its tender thought, overflowing with joy and love, rushing exuberantly into being, seemed to fall over itself and break itself in pieces.

When the girl had finished her simple but charming song, her Mozartian or shepherd girl's aria, I went up to her, greeted her, asked her for permission to congratulate her on her beautiful voice, and complimented her on her extraordinarily spiritual performance.

The little songstress, who looked like a doe, or a sort of antelope in girl's form, looked at me with her beautiful brown eyes full of questioning surprise. She had a very delicate, gentle face, and she gave me a captivating and polite smile.

"To you," I said to her, "if you know how to train carefully and tend your rich voice, a process which will require your own intelligence as well as that of others, belongs a brilliant future and a great career; for to me you seem, I frankly and honestly confess, to be the great operatic singer of the future in person.

"You are obviously clever; you are tender and supple, and if my suppositions do not entirely deceive me, you possess a most decidedly courageous soul. You have fire, and an evident nobility of heart—this I just heard in the song which you sang really beautifully and well. You have talent, but more: you have genius!

"I speak no vain or untrue words. Instead, I take it upon myself to ask you to pay your noble gift special attention, to diligently preserve it from deformity, mutilation, thoughtless premature exhaustion, and neglect. At present, I can only tell you in all sincerity that you sing exceedingly well, which is something very serious, for it means a great deal. It means above all that you will be expected industriously to sing further every day.

"Practice and sing with wise moderation. The scope and extent of the treasure in your possession you yourself certainly know not at all.

"In your vocal accomplishment there sounds already a high degree of natural grace, a rich sum of unsuspecting vigorous being, and an abundance of poetry and humanity, and for all this it seems necessary to give you positive assurance that you promise to become in every way a genuine singer. It is likely that you are a person who is compelled to sing by her very inmost nature, who appears only to live, and only to be able to enjoy life, when she begins to sing, thus transforming all her life-force and actual delight in life into the art of song, whence all that is humanly and personally significant, all that is suffused with soul, all that is full of understanding, ascends into something higher, into an ideal.

"In a beautiful song there is always a concentration and compression of experience, perception, an explosive aggregate of condensed, feeling life and animation of the soul, and with such a song, a woman who makes good use of favorable circumstances and mounts the ladder of numerous, peculiar opportunities, may as a star in the firmament of music move profoundly the hearts of many people, amass great wealth, transport a public to demonstrations of stormy, enthusiastic applause, and draw down upon herself the love and sincere admiration of kings and of queens."

Solemn, and astonished, the girl listened to my words, though I uttered them certainly more for my own delight than in any hope that the little thing might appreciate or understand them, for she lacked the necessary maturity.

From afar I can already see a railway crossing which I shall have to traverse; but, at present, I have not got that far. As must be clearly realized, I have two or three important commissions to execute, as well as several utterly insuperable arrangements to make. About these a report must be drawn up in as much detail as possible.

It will generously be permitted me to remark that I have in passing to present myself with all expediency at an elegant gentleman's outfitters or tailor's workshop to discuss a new suit which I must try on and have tailored. Second, I have to pay off heavy taxes in the local office or town hall. Third, I ought to take a noteworthy letter to the post office and throw it into the letter box. Moreover I must, after a relatively long delay, perhaps once more have my hair cut.

It will be seen how much I have to do, and how this apparently idle, easygoing walk is virtually teeming with practical business affairs. People will therefore be so good as to excuse my loitering, appreciate my delays, and approve the long-winded discussions with clerical and other professional people; yes, perhaps even welcome them as acceptable contributions and adjuncts to the entertainment. For all consequent lengths, breadths, and heights I humbly request in advance the reader's pardon.

Has a provincial or metropolitan author ever been more diffident and courteous toward the circle of his readers? I hardly think so, and therefore, with my conscience utterly clear, I continue my little chat and narrative and report the following:

God bless my soul! It's high time I went over to Frau Aebi for my dinner, or lunch. This very minute it is striking half past twelve. As luck would have it, the lady lives very near indeed to where I am standing; I need only slip, smooth as an eel, into the house, as into a loophole, and as into a shelter for poor starvelings and pitiful distressed gentlefolk.

My punctuality was a masterpiece. It is known how rare masterpieces are. Frau Aebi received me most magnanimously, smiling really most kindly, offering me, in a cordial way, which in a manner of speaking enchanted me, her nice little hand, and leading me at once into the dining room, where she requested me to sit at the table, a request which I with the utmost conceivable pleasure, and completely without restraint, fulfilled.

Without making the least ridiculous fuss, I began harmlessly to eat and to help myself without reserve, a long way from guessing what was in store for me.

Anyway, I began boldly to help myself and stoutly to eat, for such boldness, as is well known, costs not much in the way of sacrifice. With some surprise, however, I observed that Frau Aebi was watching me with something like devotion. This was quite noticeable. Obviously, it moved her deeply to watch how I helped myself and ate. This curious situation astonished me; but I attributed no major significance to it.

The moment I wanted to supply a little conversation and diversion, Frau Aebi stopped me and said that she declined all forms of conversation with the greatest pleasure. This curious phrase took me aback; I began to be anxious and afraid. Secretly I began to be terrified in Frau Aebi's presence. When I wanted to stop cutting it up and popping it in, because I felt that I was full, she said to me in a delicate manner and tone of voice, through which gently shuddered a maternal rebuke:

"But you are not eating! Wait, I'll cut you another big juicy slice."

A sense of dread rippled through me. Politely and courteously I ventured to object that my main purpose in coming here had been to deploy a certain intellectuality, whereupon Frau Aebi, smiling most captivatingly, said that she did not think this to be at all necessary.

"I cannot possibly go on eating," I said, in a dull muffled voice. I was almost suffocating, and was already perspiring with terror. Frau Aebi said:

"I absolutely cannot believe that you want to stop cutting it up and popping it in, and I do not think that you are really full at all. When you say that you are just about suffocating, you are quite definitely not telling the truth. I am compelled to consider that as mere politeness. I decline any form of intellectual chat, as I said before, with pleasure. Certainly your main purpose in coming here was to prove that you're a big eater and demonstrate that you have a good appetite. This consideration I cannot under any circumstances forgo; rather, I would cordially ask you to be sensible and accommodate yourself to the inevitable; for I can assure you that there is no possibility that you will leave this table before you have eaten up and polished off everything that I have cut, and will cut, off for you.

"I am afraid you are helplessly vanquished, for you must realize that there are housewives who compel their guests to help themselves and pack themselves to the brim, until they burst. A lamentable, deplorable fate awaits you; but you must endure it bravely. Each of us in due course has to make some great sacrifice!

"So obey and eat. For to obey surely is sweet. What harm can it do if you perish in the attempt? Here, this most delicate, delicious, large slice you must certainly demolish, I know you will. Courage, my good friend! We all need to be brave. What worth are we, if we persist forever steadfast in our own will?

"Concentrate all your strength, and compel yourself to do the loftiest deed, to endure the most difficult trial, and to survive the most arduous struggle.

"You cannot believe how glad I am to watch you eat till you drop unconscious. You cannot imagine how disappointed I would be if you were to refuse me this—but you will do it, won't you? You'll bite your best and help yourself, won't you, even if you are so full that your back teeth are floating?"

"Terrible woman! What do you want with me?" I exclaimed and sprang up from the table and made as if to rush out and away. Frau Aebi, however, held me back, laughed aloud and cordially, and confessed that she had permitted herself a joke with me, which I would please be so good as not to grudge her.

"I only wanted to give you an example of how it is done by certain housewives, who almost overflow with kindness toward their guests."

At this I had to laugh to myself, and I may admit that in her exuberance I liked Frau Aebi very much. She wanted to have me near her the whole afternoon, and was almost a little indignant when I told her that it was, unfortunately for me, an impossible thing for me to afford her my company any longer, because I had to settle certain important affairs, which I absolutely could not put off. It was extremely flattering to me to hear Frau Aebi so vigorously regretting that I had to run off again so soon and wanted to. She asked me if it was really so pressingly urgent to abscond and vanish, whereupon I gave her the most holy assurances that only the most pressing urgency had the ability and power to draw me away so soon from such a pleasant house and from such an attractive, esteemed person, words with which I look my leave of her.

It was now meet to conquer, master, surprise, and abash in his utterly unshakable convictions an obstinate, recalcitrant tailor, or *marchand tailleur*, a person obviously in every respect convinced of the infallibility of his doubtless eminent skill, as well as completely saturated with a sense of his own efficiency.

The toppling of a master tailor's fixity of mind must be considered one of the most difficult and hazardous tasks which courage can undertake and daredevil determination determine to carry forward. Of tailors and their opinions I have a comprehensive, constant, and intense fear, of which, however, I am not at all ashamed, for fear is, in this instance, readily explicable.

So I was, then, prepared for trouble, perhaps even for trouble of the worst kind, and I armed myself for such a highly perilous attack with qualities such as courage, scorn, wrath, indignation, disdain, even the disdain of death; and with these indubitably very appreciable weapons I hoped to advance, victoriously and successfully, against biting irony and mockery lurking under a simulation of friendliness.

It turned out otherwise, however. But I will be silent on this point till later, particularly as first I still have to dispatch a letter. For I have just decided to go first to the post office, then to the tailor, and after this to pay my taxes.

Besides, the post office, a tasteful building, lay right in front of my nose. Blithely I went in and besought the responsible post office official for a stamp, which I stuck upon the envelope.

While I then circumspectly slipped the same down into the letter box, I examined and weighed pensively, in my mind, what I had written. As I very well knew, the contents were as follows:

"Most respectable Sir,

"The curious form of address should bring you the assurance that the writer confronts you utterly coldly. I know that respect of myself is not to be expected from you, nor from any persons of your sort, for the reason that you and persons of your sort have an exorbitant opinion of themselves, which allows them to achieve neither understanding nor any sort of discretion. I know with certainty that you are one of those people who appear to themselves important because they are inconsiderate and discourteous, who think themselves powerful because they enjoy protection, who believe themselves wise because the little word 'wise' happens now and then to occur to them.

"People like you are so bold as to be hard, coarse, impudent, and violent with regard to people who are poor and unprotected. People like you possess the unorthodox wit to believe that it is necessary to be everywhere on top, to keep everywhere the ascendancy, and to triumph at every moment of the day. People like you do not observe that this is foolish and that it neither lies within the bounds of possibility nor is in any way to be desired. People like you are snobs and are ready at all times industriously to serve brutality. People like you are exceedingly courageous in the evasion of any sort of genuine courage, because they know that this true courage promises to injure them; furthermore they are courageous in always demonstrating with an uncommon degree of pleasure and an uncommon degree of zeal their right to set up as the good and the beautiful. People like you respect neither old age nor merit, and certainly not hard work. People like you respect money, and respect of this sort obstructs any higher estimation of other things.

"He who works honestly, and devotedly exerts himself, is in the eyes of people like you, an outspoken ass. In this I do not err; for my little finger can tell me that I am right. I must dare to tell you to your face that you abuse your position because you know full well how many annoyances and tedious complications would be entailed if anyone were to rap your knuckles. In the grace and favor which you enjoy, ensconced in your privileged prescriptive position, you are still wide open to attack, for you feel without a doubt how insecure you are.

"You betray confidence, do not keep your word, injure without a second thought the virtues and reputations of those who have to deal with you; you rob unsparingly where you pretend to institute beneficence, impose upon the services and denigrate the person of every servant, you are fickle and unreliable, and show qualities which one might willingly pardon in a girl, but not in a man.

"Forgive me if I allow myself to think you exceedingly weak, and accept, with the candid assurance that he would consider it advisable to avoid any future contact with you in his affairs, the required measure and the established degree of respect from a person upon whom devolved both the distinction and the inevitably moderate pleasure of having been permitted to make your acquaintance."

I almost regretted that I had entrusted to the post for dispatch and delivery this cutthroat's letter, as it now subsequently appeared to me: indeed, to no less than a leading, influential personality I had in such an ideal manner proclaimed, thus conjuring up a furious state of war, the rupture of diplomatic or, better, economic relations. Still, I unleashed my challenge, while I consoled myself with the reflection that this personality, or most respectable sir, would in all likelihood scarcely read my communication even once, let alone several times, since, on perusing and relishing even the second or third word of this delicious piece of writing, he would probably have had quite enough, causing him presumably to hurl the blazing effusion, without losing much time or precious energy about it, into his all-devouring, all-accommodating wastepaper basket.

"Besides, in the course of nature, a thing like this is forgotten in six or three months," I concluded and philosophized and marched, *bravement*, to my tailor.

The same sat happily, and with what seemed the clearest conscience in the world, in his elegant fashion salon or workshop crammed with subtly fragrant rolls and remnants of cloth. A cage-imprisoned, blustering bird, along with a keen crafty apprentice nicely occupied with cutting out, and seemingly intended to complete the idyllic scene.

Herr Dünn the master tailor rose as he caught sight of me most courteously from his seat, where he had been diligently fencing with his needle, to bid the visitor a friendly welcome.

"You have come about your suit, an unquestionably impeccable fit, which is soon to be delivered complete and finished by my firm," he said, as he tendered me, well-nigh all too companionably, his hand, which I nevertheless was not in the least hesitant to shake.

"I have come," I parried, "to proceed dauntlessly and full of hope to the fitting, though I have my fears."

Herr Dünn said that he considered fears of any sort to be superfluous, since he guaranteed both the fit and the cut.

As he was saying this, he led me into an adjoining room, from which he himself at once withdrew. That he repeatedly guaranteed and protested did not quite please me especially. The fitting, along with the disappointment which was so intimately connected with it, was soon complete.

Straining to fight back an overflowing chagrin, I shouted loudly and energetically for Herr Dünn, at whom, with possibly great composure and genteel dissatisfaction, I flung the unquestionably annihilating outburst:

"It's exactly as I thought!"

"My dear and most esteemed sir, it is useless to excite yourself."

Laboriously enough I brought out: "There is assuredly cause enough and plenty to spare that I should get excited and be inconsolable. Kindly keep your highly inept attempts at appeasement to yourself and be so good as to upset me no longer. What you have done in the way of making a faultless suit is in the highest degree upsetting. All the delicate or indelicate fears that arose in me have been justified in every respect, and my worst expectations have been fulfilled in every way. How can you dare to guarantee a faultless cut and fit, and how is it possible that you have the audacity to assure me that you are a master in your craft, when you must confess, even with only a very sparse measure of honesty and with only the smallest degree of perceptiveness and honorable dealing, that I am entirely displeased and that the faultless suit to be delivered to me by your esteemed, excellent firm is completely botched?"

"I must courteously disallow the term 'botched'."

"I will control my feelings, Herr Dünn."

"I thank you and am cordially delighted by such a pleasant resolve."

"You will allow me to expect of you that you make considerable and incisive alterations to this suit, which, as evidenced by the recent fitting, reveals entire multitudes of mistakes, defects, and blemishes."

"I might."

"Dissatisfaction, displeasure, and the grief I feel, force me to inform you that you have vexed me."

"I swear to you that I am sorry."

"The assiduity with which you choose to swear that you are sorry to have vexed me and put me in ill humor does not in the least modify the defectiveness of the suit, to which I vehemently refuse to accord even the smallest degree of recognition, and acceptance of which I vigorously reject, as there can be no question of either approbation or applause.

"As regards the jacket, I clearly feel that it makes me a hunchback, and consequently hideous, deformation with which I can under no circumstances concur. On the contrary, I emphatically protest.

"The sleeves suffer from a positively objectionable overabundance of length. The waistcoat is eminently distinguished in that it creates the nasty impression and evokes the unpleasant semblance of my being the bearer of a fat stomach.

"The trousers are absolutely disgusting. Their design or scheme inspires me with a genuine feeling of horror. Where this miserable, ridiculous, and terrifyingly idiotic work of trouserly art should possess a certain breadth, it exhibits very straitlaced narrowness, and where it should be narrow, it is more than wide.

"Your execution, Herr Dünn, is in sum unimaginative. Your work manifests an absence of intelligence. There adheres to such a suit something despicable, deplorable, petty-minded, something inane, fearful, and homemade. The man who made it can assuredly not be counted among men of spirit. Such an utter absence of talent remains in any case regrettable indeed."

Herr Dünn had the imperturbability to reply: "I do not understand your indignation, nor shall I ever be persuaded to understand you. The numerous violent reproofs which you feel obliged to heap upon me are incomprehensible to me, and will very probably remain incomprehensible. The suit fits exceedingly well. Nobody can make me think otherwise. My conviction that you appear uncommonly to your advantage in it, I declare to be unshakable. To certain distinguishing features of it you will soon become accustomed. Very high-up state officials order their estimable requirements from me. Graciously likewise do Justices of the Peace send me their commissions. This beyond all question striking proof of my capability should satisfy you! For exaggerated expectations I cannot possibly cater, and luckily, arrogant demands leave master tailor Dünn utterly cold. Better situated persons and more eminent gentlemen than you have been in every respect satisfied with my proficiency and skill, by which I would like to remark that I hope to have disarmed you."

Since I had to agree that it was impossible to accomplish anything, and considering that an alas perhaps excessively fiery, impetuous onslaught had been transformed into the most painful and ignominious of defeats, I withdrew my troops from this unfortunate engagement, broke feebly off, and flew the field in shame.

In such manner was concluded the audacious adventure with the tailor. Without another glance about me, I sped to the municipal treasury, to settle my taxes. Here, however, a gross error must be corrected.

That is to say, as it now subsequently occurs to me, it was a question less of payment than merely, for the time being, of a discussion with the President of the laudable Commission for Revenues, and of the handing in, or handing over, of a solemn declaration. May my readers not hold this error against me, but listen generously to what I have to say in this connection.

As adequately as the resolute master tailor Dünn guaranteed faultlessness, so do I promise and guarantee, with regard to the declaration to be rendered, exactitude and completeness, as well as concision and brevity.

With a bound I enter the charming situation in question:

"Permit me to inform you," I said frankly and freely to the tax man—or high, respectable revenue official—who gave me his governmental ear in order to follow attentively the report I was about to deliver, "that I enjoy, as a poor writer or *homme de lettres*, a very dubious income.

"It is self-evident that you will not find in my case the tiniest trace of an amassed fortune, as I here affirm with deep regret, without, however, shedding any tears over the unfortunate fact.

"Despair I do not, but just as little can I exult or rejoice. I generally get along as best I can, as they say.

"I dispense with all luxuries. A single glance at my person should tell you this. The food I eat can be described as sufficient and frugal.

"It apparently occurred to you to consider that I might have at my disposal many sources of income. I feel myself, however, compelled to oppose, courteously but decisively, this belief along with all such suppositions, and to tell the simple unadorned truth, which is, in any case, that I am extremely free from wealth, but, on the other hand, laden with every sort of poverty, as you might be so kind as to write in your notebook.

"On Sundays I may scarcely allow myself to be seen on the streets, for I have no Sunday clothes. In my steady, thrifty way of life I am like a field mouse. Even a sparrow seems to have better prospects of prosperity than this deliverer of a report and taxpayer you see before you. I have written several books, which unfortunately were quite poorly received by the reading public, and the consequences of this oppress my heart. Not for a moment do I doubt that you understand this, and that you will consequently realize my peculiar financial situation.

"Ordinary civil status, civil esteem, etc. I by no means possess; that's as clear as daylight. Toward men such as myself, no sense of obligation seems to exist. Exceedingly few persons profess a lively interest in literature. Besides, the pitiless criticism of our work, which any manjack thinks himself obliged to practice, constitutes yet another abundant hurt that, like a drag chain, drags down the aspirant accomplisher of a state of modest wellbeing.

"Certainly there exist amicable patrons and friendly patronesses, who subsidize the poet nobly from time to time. But a gift is far from being income, and a subsidy is surely no fortune.

"For all these I hope convincing reasons, most honored sir, I would request you kindly to overlook all the increases in taxation which you have communicated to me, and in God's name to set your rate of taxation in my case at as low a level as possible."

The superintendent or inspector of taxes said: "But you're always to be seen out for a walk!"

"Walk," was my answer, "I definitely must, to invigorate myself and to maintain contact with the living world, without perceiving which I could neither write the half of one more single word, nor produce a poem in verse or prose. Without walking, I would be dead, and would have long since been forced to abandon my profession, which I love passionately. Also, without walking and gathering reports, I would not be able to render the tiniest report, nor to produce an essay, let alone a story. Without walking, I would be able to collect neither observations nor studies. Such a clever, enlightened man as you will understand this at once.

"On a far-wandering walk a thousand usable thoughts occur to me, while shut in at home, I would lamentably wither and dry up. Walking is for me not only healthy, it is also of service—not only lovely, but also useful. A walk advances me professionally, but also provides me at the same time with amusement; it comforts, delights, and refreshes me, is a pleasure for me, but also has the peculiarity that it spurs me on and allures me to further creation, since it offers me as material numerous more or less significant objectivities upon which I can later work industriously at home. Every walk is filled with phenomena valuable to see and feel. A pleasant walk most often veritably teems with imageries, living poems, attractive objects, natural beauties, be they ever so small. The lore of nature and the lore of the country are revealed, charming and graceful, to the sense and eyes of the observant walker, who must of course walk not with downcast but with open, unclouded eyes, if he desires the lovely significance and the broad, noble idea of the walk to dawn on him.

"Consider how the poet would have to grow impoverished and run sadly to ruin if that maternal, paternal, child-like, beautiful nature did not ever and again reacquaint him with the source of the good and of the beautiful. Consider the great unabating importance for the poet of the instruction and golden holy teaching which he derives out there in the play of the open air. Without walking and the contemplation of nature which is connected with it, without this equally delicious and instructive, equally refreshing and constantly admonishing search, I deem myself lost, and indeed am lost. With the utmost attention and love the man who walks must study and observe every smallest living thing, be it a child, a dog, a fly, a butterfly, a sparrow, a worm, a flower, a man, a house, a tree, a hedge, a snail, a mouse, a cloud, a hill, a leaf, or no more than a paltry discarded scrap of paper on which, perhaps, a dear good child at school has written his first clumsy letters.

"The highest and lowest, most serious as well as most hilarious things are to him equally beloved, beautiful, and valuable. He must bring with him no sort of sentimentally sensitive self-love, but rather he must let his careful eye wander and stroll where it will, unselfish and unegoistic, must continuously be able to efface himself in the contemplation and observation of things, while understanding how to put behind him, little consider, and forget outright like a brave, zealous, and joyfully self-immolating front-line soldier, himself, his private complaints, needs, wants, and sacrifices.

"If he does not, then he walks with only half his spirit, which is not worth much.

"Of compassion, sympathy, and enthusiasm he must at all times be capable—and it is hoped that he is. He must be able to launch himself up into enthusiasm but just as easily sink down into the smallest everyday thing—and it is probable that he can. Faithful, devoted self-surrender and self-effacement among objects, and assiduous love for all phenomena, also make him happy, however, just as every performance of duty make that man rich and happy in his inmost being who is aware of his duty. Spirit and devotion bless him, raise him high up above his own walking self, which has only too often a name for non-utilitarian, time-wasting vagabondage. Manifold studies enrich, hearten, appease, and ennoble him, and moreover what he is so diligently practicing may touch the fringes of exact science, a thing of which nobody would think the apparently frivolous wanderer capable.

"Do you realize that I am working obstinately and tenaciously with my brain, and am often perhaps in the best sense active when I present the appearance of a simultaneously heedless and out-of-work, negligent, dreamy, idle pickpocket, lost out in the blue, or in the green, making a bad impression, apparently devoid of any sense of responsibility?

"Mysterious there prowl at the walker's heels all kinds of thoughts and notions, such as make him stand in his ardent and regardless tracks and listen, because, again and again confused by curious impressions, by spirit power, he suddenly has the bewitching feeling that he is sinking into the earth, for an abyss has opened before the dazzled, bewildered eyes of the thinker and poet. His head wants to fall off. His otherwise so lively arms and legs are as benumbed. Countryside and people, sounds and colors, faces and farms, clouds and sunlight swirl all around him like diagrams; he asks himself: "Where am I?"

"Earth and heaven stream together and collide, rocking flashing interlocked one upon the other into an obscurely shimmering nebular imagery. Chaos begins and the orders vanish. Convulsed, he laboriously tries to retain his state of mind; he succeeds. Later he walks on, full of confidence.

"Do you think it quite impossible that on a patient walk like this I should meet giants, have the privilege of

seeing professors, do business in passing with booksell-
ers and bank officials, converse with budding youthful
songstresses and former actresses, dine at noon with
intelligent ladies, stroll through woods, dispatch danger-
ous letters, and come to wild blows with spiteful, ironic
master tailors? All this can happen, after all, and I believe
it actually did happen.

"There accompanies the walker always something
remarkable, something fantastic, and he would be foolish if he wished to let this spiritual side go unnoticed; by
no means, however, does he do this, but rather cordially
welcomes all peculiar phenomena, becomes their friend,
their brother; he makes them into formed and substantial
bodies, gives them soul and structure just as they too for
their part instruct and inspire him.

"In short: by thinking, pondering, drilling, digging,
speculating, writing, investigating, researching, and
walking, I earn my daily bread with as much sweat on
my brow as anybody. Although I may cut a most carefree
figure, I am highly serious and conscientious, and though
I seem to be no more than dreamy and delicate, I am a
solid technician! Might I hope, through the meticulous
explanations I have brought forth, to have convinced you
completely of the obviously honorable nature of these
endeavors?"

The official said: "Good!" and added: "Your application

concerning approval of an exceptionally low rate of taxation shall be examined later. You shall be informed shortly of the reduction or approval thereof as may be. For the kind declaration delivered as well as for the industriously assembled honest statements we thank you very much. For the present you may withdraw in order to proceed nicely with your walk."

As I was mercifully released, I hurried happily away, and was soon thereafter in the open air again, where delight and the raptures of freedom seized me and carried me away.

After many a bravely endured adventure, and after more or less victoriously overwhelming many an obstacle, I come at last to the long-since forecast railway crossing. Here I had to stop a while to wait pleasantly until gradually the train kindly had something like the high grace to pass gently by. All sorts of male and female folk of every age and character were standing and waiting at the barrier, as did I. The kindly, corpulent signalman's wife examined us waiters and loiterers thoroughly. Hurtling past, the railway train was full of soldiery. All the soldiers rendering service to their dearly beloved fatherland, looking out at the windows on the one hand, and the useless civilian population on the other, greeted each other gaily and patriotically, an action which spread pleasant feelings far and wide.

When the crossing was open, I and all the others went peacefully on our ways, and now all the world around seemed to me suddenly to be a thousand times more beautiful. My walk was becoming more beautiful and long. Here at the railway crossing seemed to be something like the peak, or the center, from which again the gentle declivity would begin, I thought to myself. Already I sensed something like the just-beginning, gentle slope of evening. Something akin to sorrow's bliss breathed around me as a quiet, lofty god. "It is divinely beautiful here," I thought again.

The gentle countryside with its dear humble fields, houses, and gardens seemed to me like a sweet song of departure. Everywhere thronged resounding, ancient lamentations of a poor folk and their sorrows. Spirits with enchanting garments emerged, vast, soft, vague figures. The dainty, beautiful country road shone sky-blue, white, and gold. Above the dun-colored, rosy-aureoled houses of the poor—which the sunlight delicately, childishly embraced—compassion and enchantment flew like carven angels falling from heaven. Hand in hand in their rarefied breath love and poverty floated. I felt as if someone were calling me by name, or as if someone were kissing and soothing me; God himself, the Almighty, our merciful Lord and master, walked down the road, to make it indescribably beautiful. Imaginings of all sorts bid me believe that Jesus Christ had come here and was wandering now in the midst of all the good, dear people and in the midst of this charming place. All that was human and solid seemed to be transfigured into a soul filled with gentleness. Veils of silver soul-haze swam through all things and lay over all things. The soul of the world had opened, and I fantasized that everything wicked, distressing and painful was on the point of vanishing. Earlier walks came before my eyes. But the wonderful image of the present swiftly became a feeling which overpowered all others. All notion of the future paled and the past dissolved. In the glowing present I myself glowed. From every direction and distance, all things great and good emerged brightly with marvelous, uplifting gestures. In the midst of this beautiful place, I thought of nothing but this place itself; all other thoughts sank away. Attentively I looked only at what was most slight and most humble, while the heavens seemed to incline far up into the heights and down into the depths. The earth became a dream; I myself had become an inward being, and I walked as in an inward world. Everything outside me faded to obscurity, and all I had understood till now was unintelligible. I fell away from the surface, down into the depths, which I recognized then to be all that was good. What we understand and love understands and loves us also. I was no longer myself, I was another, yet it was on this account that I became properly myself. In the sweet light of love I believed I was able to recognize—or required to feel—that the inward self is the only self which really exists. The thought seized me: "Where would we humans be, if there was no good earth faithful to us? What would we have, if we were lacking this? Where would I be, if I was not here? Here I have everything, and elsewhere I would have nothing."

What I saw was as poor as it was large, as small as it was significant, as charming as it was modest, and as good as it was warm and delightful. Two houses which lay like lively and kindly neighbors, close together in the bright sunlight, delighted me especially. In the soft confiding air floated one contentment after the other, trembling as with quiet joy. One of the two houses was the Bear Inn. Admirably and comically, I found, was the bear depicted on the inn sign. Chestnut trees overshadowed the delicate house, which was assuredly inhabited by pleasant, kind people; it did not seem, like some buildings, to be arrogant, but rather the very image of intimacy and trust. Everywhere the eye looked lay splendid profusion of gardens, hung green tangled profusion of pleasant leaves.

The second house, in its evident delightfulness and humility, was like a childishly beautiful page out of a picture book, so curious and charming did it show itself to be. The vicinity of the cottage seemed entirely beautiful and good.

I fell immediately head over heels in love with this pretty little house person, and I would have passionately liked to go into it at once, in order to make my nest and lodging there and to put down roots in this magic cottage, forever and content; unfortunately, however, it is just the most beautiful houses which are occupied, and the person who looks for a dwelling to suit his presumptuous tastes has a difficult time, because that which is empty and might be available is often frightful and inspires vivid horror.

Surely the pretty cottage was inhabited by a little spinster or grandmother, that's what it looked like, and it had about it just such a smell. I report, being so permitted, that on the small building abounded wall paintings or frescoes, which subtly showed a Swiss alpine landscape in which stood, amusingly painted again, a Bernese mountain farmhouse. Admittedly, the painting was not good at all. It would be impudent to maintain that it was a work of art. But, nonetheless, to me it seemed delightful. Simple and plain as it was, it even enchanted me. As a matter of fact, any sort of painting enchants me, however clumsy it is, because every painting reminds me first of diligence and industry, and second of Holland. Is not all music, even the most niggardly, beautiful to the person who loves the very being and existence of music? Is not almost any human being you please—even the worst and most unpleasant—lovable to the person who is a friend to man?

That painted landscape in the middle of real landscape is capricious, piquant nobody will contest. The fact that a little old lady may live in the house I certainly did not anyway establish on record. But I am surprised at myself that I should dare to use the word "fact" here, where all around me everything should be supple and full of nature, like the thoughts and feelings of a mother's heart! As for the rest, the cottage was painted blue-gray and had bright green shutters, which seemed to smile, and in the garden was a fragrance of most beautiful flowers. Over the little garden- and summerhouse there bowed and twisted with enchanting grace a rosebush or shrub full of lovely roses.

Assuming I am not delirious, but hale and hearty, as I vigorously hope and absolutely do not doubt I am, proceeding gently on my way I passed by a country barbershop, with whose contents and owner, however, I in fact scarcely have cause to concern myself, because I am of the opinion that it is not yet quite so urgently necessary for me to have my hair cut, though this would be perhaps quite pleasant and amusing.

Further, I passed by a cobbler's workshop, which reminded me of the unhappy poet Lenz, who learned to make, and made, shoes while in a state of mental derangement and spiritual unhingedness.

In passing I looked into a friendly schoolroom, exactly when the schoolmistress was issuing questions and loud commands, whereby it should be added how eagerly the walker for an instant wished he might once more be a child and a disobedient schoolboy, go to school again and be permitted to harvest a well-earned thrashing in punishment for naughtiness committed.

Speaking of thrashings, our opinion might here be interlarded that a countryman, if he is not hesitant to cut down the pride of the landscape, the glory of his own hearth and home, namely his high and ancient nut tree, in order to trade it in for despicable, foolish money deserves to be properly thrashed.

For, passing by a beautiful farmhouse with a splendid, luxuriant nut tree, I cried aloud: "This high majestical tree which protects and beautifies this house so wonderfully, spinning for it a cage and garment of such serious, joyous homeliness, intimate domesticity, such a tree, I say, is like a divinity, and a thousand lashes to the unfeeling owner of it if he dare make all this cool, green leafy splendor vanish just to gratify his thirst for money, which is the vilest thing on earth. Cretins of this sort should be kicked out of the parish. To Siberia or Tierra del Fuego with such defilers and destroyers of what is beautiful. But, thank God, there are also farmers who certainly still have senses and hearts for what is delicate and good."

As regards the tree, the greed, the countryman, the transportation to Siberia, and the thrashing which the

countryman apparently deserves because he fells the tree,
I have perhaps gone too far, and I must confess that I let
my indignation carry me away. Friends of beautiful trees
will nevertheless understand my displeasure, and agree
with this energetically expressed regret. For all I care, the
thousand lashes can be returned to me forthwith. To the
coarse expression "cretin" I myself deny applause. Being
compelled to dislike it, I beg the reader's forgiveness. As
I have already had to beg his forgiveness several times, I
have become quite a dab hand at courtesies of this sort.
"Unfeeling owner" I had no need at all to say. Such over-
heatings of the mind, as I see it, ought absolutely to be
avoided. It is, however, obvious that I will allow my grief
over the downfall of a beautiful tree to stand. I certainly
make the worst of it; nobody shall hinder me from that.
"Kicked out of the parish" is an improvident phrase, and
as for the thirst for money, which I have called vile, I
suppose that I have myself at some time or another of-
fended, fallen short, and sinned in this respect, and that
certain wretchednesses and vilenesses have certainly not
remained alien to me.

I here implement a policy of softheartedness, which
has a beauty that is not to be found anywhere else; but
I consider a policy of this sort to be indispensable. Pro-
priety enjoins us to be careful to deal as severely with
ourselves as with others, to judge others as mildly as we

judge ourselves, which latter we do, as is well known, at all times instinctively.

It is delicious, is it not, the way mistakes are being corrected here and offenses smoothed over? In making admissions I prove myself peace-loving, and in rounding off the angles, evening out the bumps, and making soft what is rough I am a subtle attenuator, show a sense of good tone, and am most tidily diplomatic. Of course I have disgraced myself; yet I hope that my good will at least is appreciated.

If anybody still says now that I am indiscreet, imperious, and a despot blundering about at will, then I maintain that the person who says such a thing is sorely mistaken. With such continual gentility and considerateness, most probably no other author has ever thought of the reader.

Well, now I can obligingly attend to a château and aristocratic palace, and as follows:

I politely play my trump card, for with a half-ruined stately home and patrician house, age-gray, park-surrounded proud knight's castle and lordly residence such as now enters my view, one can make a great song and dance, excite respect, arouse envy, inspire wonder, and pocket the proceeds.

Many a poor, elegant man of letters would live with the greatest of pleasure, the highest satisfaction, in a castle, or stronghold, with courtyard and drive for haughty carriages embossed with coats-of-arms. Many a pleasure-loving, poor painter dreams of residing temporarily on delicious old-fashioned country estates. Many a city girl, educated but unfortunately, it seems, poor as a church mouse, thinks with melancholy rapture and idealistic fervor of ponds, grottoes, high chambers, and sedan chairs, and of herself waited upon by hurrying footmen and noble-minded knights.

On the lordly residence I saw before me, that is, rather in it than on it, could be both seen and read the date 1709, which naturally quickened and intensified my interest. With a curiosity nearly verging on rapture I looked as a naturalist and antiquary into the dreaming, ancient, curious garden, where, in a pool with a pleasant splashing fountain, I discovered with ease a most peculiar fish, which was one meter in length; namely, a solitary sheat-fish. Likewise I saw and established with romantic bliss the presence of a garden pavilion in Moorish or Arabian style, opulently painted in sky-blue, with mysterious stars, brown, and serious noble black. With the most subtle intelligence, I sensed at once that the pavilion must have been erected in about the year 1858, a deduction, conjecture, and scenting-out which possibly on occasion entitles me confidently to read with a rather complacent expression on my face, and in a rather self-confident manner, a pertinent paper on the subject in the Town Hall Chambers, before a large and enthusiastic public. Then very probably the press would mention my lecture, which could only mean an extreme pleasure for me—since sometimes it mentions all sorts of things with not even one small dying word, which is in fact just what occurred.

As I was studying intently the Persian garden pavilion, it occurred to me to think: "How beautiful it must be here at night when, veiled in an almost impenetrable darkness, everything all around is quiet, black, and soundless, pines gently towering out of the darkness, midnight awe arrests the solitary wanderer, and now a lamp, which spreads a sweet yellow light, is brought into the pavilion by a richly jeweled woman, who then, moved by her peculiar whim and by a curious access of soul, begins, at the piano, with which in this case our summerhouse must naturally be equipped, to play music to which, if the dream be permitted, she sings in a delightfully beautiful voice, so that one cannot help but listen and dream and be made happy by this night music."

But it was not midnight and far and wide neither a courtly Middle Ages, nor any year 1500 or 1700, but broad daylight and a working day, and a troupe of people—together with a most uncourtly, unknightly, most crude, most impertinent automobile, which came my way—rudely disturbed me at my wealth of learned observations, and threw me in a trice out of the domain of castle poetry and reverie on things past, so that I cried out instinctively:

"It really is shockingly vulgar the way people impede

me here from making my elegant studies and from plunging into the most superb profundities. While I have grounds for indignation, I would rather be meek and endure with a good grace; thoughts of bygone beauty and loveliness, and the pale image of sunken nobility may well be sweet; but on the world around and on one's fellow men one will not therefore have cause to turn one's back. One cannot possibly talk oneself into believing that one is entitled to resent people and their contrivances because they disregard the state of mind of him whose desire it is to be absorbed in the realms of history and thought.

"A thunderstorm," I thought as I walked on, "would no doubt be magnificent here. I hope I shall have the opportunity to experience one."

An honest jet-black dog who lay in the road I honored with the following facetious address:

"Does it not enter your mind, you apparently quite unschooled, uncultivated fellow, to stand up and offer me a greeting, though you can see at once from my gait as well as the rest of my conduct that I am a person who has lived a full seven years in cosmopolitan capitals, and who during this time has not one minute, let alone one hour, or one month, or one week, been out of most pleasant touch with exclusively cultured and important people? Where, ragamuffin, were you brought up? And you do not answer me a word? You lie where you are, look at me impertinently, move not a finger, as motionless as a monument? What boorish conduct!"

Yet actually I liked the dog in his loyal-hearted, humorous repose and composure uncommonly well, and, because his eyes twinkled at me merrily, no doubt grasping not a word of what I said, I could venture to scold him, which however, as will have been made abundantly clear by the comic manner of my address, I cannot in any way have meant unkindly.

Catching sight of an elegant, well-starched gentleman strutting, waddling and prancing toward me, I had the melancholy thought: "Is it possible that such a magnificently attired, elaborately groomed, splendidly tailored, upholstered, beringed and jewel-behung, spick-and-span beau of a gentleman does not give a moment's thought to poor, little, ill-dressed, disheveled young creatures who go about often enough in rags, show a sad lack of attention, and are lamentably neglected? Is the peacock not a little uneasy? Does this Adult Gentleman not feel in any way whatsoever concerned when he sees stained, disheveled youth? How can mature men want to walk about adorned while there are children who have no finery to wear at all?"

But one might perhaps have just as much right to say that nobody ought to go to concerts, or visit the theater, or enjoy any other kind of amusement as long as there are places of punishment in the world with unhappy prisoners in them. This is of course asking too much; for if anyone were to postpone contentment until he were to find no more poverty or misery anywhere, then he would be waiting until the impenetrable end of all time, and until the gray, ice-cold empty end of the world, and by then all joie de vivre would in all probability be utterly gone from him.

A disheveled, discomfited, spent, and tremulous charwoman, extraordinarily weak and weary, and nevertheless hurrying along because she evidently still had many more things to do, reminded me for an instant of pampered little girls (or larger girls) who often seem not to know what sort of delicate elegant occupation or diversion to pass the day with, who perhaps are never thoroughly tired, who consider all day and for weeks on end what they can do to increase the polish of their appearance, who have time and to spare for elaborate meditations on the subject, whence more and more exaggerated refinements wrap round their persons and sweet confection-like little forms.

But I am myself usually a lover and admirer of such amiable, utterly pampered moonbeam maidens, delicate, beautiful, plantlike girls. A charming young thing could almost command of me whatever she wanted, I would blindly obey her. How beautiful beauty is, and how charming is charm!

Once more I return to the topic of architecture and building, and here a bit, or spot, of literature will need consideration.

But first a note: the decking out of ancient, noble, dignified, historic places and buildings with tawdry flowers and other ornamentation reveals considerable bad taste. Whoever does this, or causes it to be done, sins against the spirit of dignity and beauty, and injures the remembrance of ancestors, who were as brave as they were noble.

Second, never conceal and garland the architecture of fountains with flowers, which of course are in themselves beautiful, but certainly do not exist to declarify and erase the noble austerity, the rigorous beauty of images in stone. At any time the predilection for flowers can deteriorate into a decidedly foolish mania. In this, as in other matters, moderation should be the goal. Personalities, such as magistrates and so forth may, if they would be so kind and perhaps do so, nicely make inquiries at any time in the authoritative circles and thereafter be good enough to behave accordingly.

To mention two interesting edifices, which arrested me to an unusually high degree, it may be reported that as I followed my road farther I came to a curious chapel, which I immediately named Brentano's Chapel, because I saw that it dated from the fantastical, radiantly aureoled, half-bright and half-dark Romantic age. I recalled Brentano's great, wild, tempestuous novel *Godwi*. Lofty, slender, arched windows gave this original building a peculiar, delightful, delicate appearance, and laid upon it the spirit of inwardness and the enchantment of meditative life. There came to my mind fiery, profound landscape descriptions by the very poet mentioned above, particularly the account of German oak forests.

Soon after this I was standing in front of a villa called Terrasse, which reminded me of the painter Karl Stauffer-Bern, who lived here for a time, and, simultaneously, of certain dainty, superb edifices which lie on the Tiergartenstrasse in Berlin, and, owing to the majestical, simple classical style to which they give expression, are congenial and worth seeing.

To me, both Stauffer's House and Brentano's Chapel were monuments to two worlds which are to be strictly distinguished from each other, each being in a curious way graceful, entertaining, and significant: Here a measured, cool elegance, there the exuberant, deep-minded dream; here something subtle and beautiful, there something subtle and beautiful, but in substance and structure completely different from the other, although each lies near to the other in point of time.

Upon my walk, as it incidentally appears to me, evening is gradually beginning to fall. Its quiet end, I think, cannot any more be very far away.

Perhaps this is just the place for a few everyday things and street events, each in its turn: A splendid piano factory and also several other factories and company buildings; an avenue of poplars close beside a black river; men, women, children; electric trams croaking along, each with a responsible field marshal or general peering out; a troupe of charmingly checkered and spotted pale-colored cows; peasant women on farm carts, and the rolling of wheels and cracking of whips thereto appertaining; several heavily laden, high-towering beer wagons with beer barrels; homeward-bound workers streaming and storming out of the factories; the overwhelming sight and actuality of such a mass, and the relevant curious thoughts; goods wagons with goods, coming from the goods station; an entire traveling, wandering circus with elephants, horses, dogs, zebras, giraffes, fierce lions locked in lion cages, with Singhalese, Indians, tigers, monkeys, and creepy-crawly crocodiles, girl rope dancers and polar bears, and all the requisite opulence of camp followers, servants, packs of performers and staff; further: boys armed with wooden rifles, imitating the European War as they unleash all the furies of war, a small scoundrel singing the song "One Hundred Thousand Frogs," of which he is mightily proud; further: foresters and woodsmen with trucks full of wood, two or three splendid pigs, whereat the eternally lively imagination of the observer as greedily as possible paints him a picture of the deliciousness and acceptability of a marvelously redolent, already roast joint of pork, which is understandable; a farmhouse with a motto over the entrance; two Bohemian, Galician, Slav, Wend, or even gypsy girls with red boots, jet-black eyes and ditto hair, at the sight of whom one involuntarily thinks of the plummy novel *The Gypsy Princess*, which actually happens in Hungary, though it's scarcely noticeable, or of *Preziosa*, which admittedly is of Spanish origin, but there is no need at all to take it literally.

Further, in the way of shops: paper, meat, clock, shoe, hat, iron, cloth, grocery, spice, fancy goods, millinery, bakery, and confectionery shops. And everywhere on all these things delicious evening sun. Further, much noise and uproar, schools and schoolteachers, the latter with weighty and dignified faces, landscapes, air and much else that is picturesque.

Further, not to be overlooked or forgotten: signs and advertisements, as: "Persil," or "Maggi's Unsurpassed Soups," or "Continental Rubber Heels Enormously Durable," or "Freehold Property for Sale," or "The Best Milk Chocolate," and I honestly know not what else. If one were to count until everything had been accurately enumerated, one would never reach the end. People with insight feel and observe this fact.

A placard or board struck me especially; it read as follows:

"FULL BOARD AND LODGING
or elegant gentlemen's *pension* recommends to elegant or at least better-off gentlemen its first-class cuisine, which is such that we can with a clear conscience say that it will not

merely gratify the most pampered palate but in addition delight the liveliest appetite. Nevertheless, preferably we decline to consider all-too-hungry stomachs.

"The culinary art we offer is adjusted to higher education, by which we hope to indicate that we are pleased to see only truly well-educated gentlemen banqueting at our tables. Rascals who drink their weekly or monthly wage, and who are thus unable to pay promptly, we have not the remotest desire to meet; rather, in respect of our honored guests, we expect consistently delicate conduct as well as pleasing manners.

"Charming, polite young ladies are in attendance at our deliciously laid, tasteful tables, which are decorated with all sorts of flowers. We make this clear, so that Prospective Gentlemen may understand that elegant behavior and really jolly and correct conduct are required of the likely resident from the moment he sets foot in our estimable, respectable establishment.

"With libertines, rowdies, boasters, and swaggerers we quite resolutely refuse all contact. Such persons who have cause to believe that they really are of this type will be so good as to remain at the greatest possible distance from our first-rate institute and kindly spare us their objectionable presences.

"On the other hand, every nice, delicate, polite, courteous, obliging, friendly, cheerful, not excessively gay but rather modest, elegant, quiet, steady, and above all solvent gentleman guest will unquestionably be in every respect welcome; he will be attended to most excellently and treated as courteously and kindly as is humanly possible; this we promise faithfully, and we intend to keep this promise continually, the pleasure is ours.

"Such a nice, charming gentleman will find at our tables delicacies whose like he would have great trouble to find anywhere else. From our exquisite cuisine proceed veritable masterpieces of culinary art, which everyone will have the occasion to prove who wishes to sample our Pension to which we heartily extend our earnest, urgent invitation at all times.

"The food which we place on our tables surpasses in quality as in quantity all reasonably healthy belief. No imagination, however strong, can even approximately conceive the delectable, luscious tidbits which we are accustomed to bring forth and display before the joyfully astonished eyes of our esteemed gentlemen diners here assembled.

"As has already been stressed, however, only gentlemen of the better type can come into consideration, and in order not only to avoid errors but also to remove doubts, we take the liberty of publishing our conception of such persons.

"In our eyes, he alone is a gentleman of the veritably better type who seethes with elegance and superiority, in other words someone who is just simply far better than the other ordinary people.

"People who are no more than ordinary do not suit us at all.

"A gentleman of the better type is, in our opinion, only he who entertains a maximal number of vain, foolish ideas about himself, who is determined to be convinced that his nose is finer and better by far than any other good sensible human nose whatsoever.

"The conduct of a gentleman of the better type clearly exhibits this peculiar prerequisite emphasized above, and it is upon this that we rely. Accordingly, whoever is merely good, upright, and honorable, but beyond this shows no important merits, should not trouble us.

"For the careful selection of exclusively the most elegant and superior gentlemen of the better type, we possess the most subtle intelligence. We can see from the gait, the tone of voice, from the way of initiating conversation, from the features of the face and the movements of the body, particularly from the clothes, the hat, the stick, the flower in the buttonhole, which either exists or does not, whether a gentleman belongs among the better gentlemen, or does not. The acumen we possess in this respect borders on magic, for which reason we make so bold as to contend that we credit ourselves with a certain genius in these matters.

"Well, now it is clear what sort of gentlemen we indicate, and if a person comes to us and we can tell from afar that he is not quite suitable for us and our institution, then we tell him: 'We very much regret, and we are sincerely sorry.'"

Two or three readers will perhaps raise a few doubts about the authenticity of such a notice, opining that it is hardly believable.

Perhaps there were a few repetitions here and there, but I would like to confess that I consider nature and human life to be a solemn and charming flow of fleeting approximations, which strikes me as a phenomenon which I believe to be beautiful and replete with blessings.

That in some places one finds sensation-hungry novelty hunters, spoiled by frequent overexcitement, who are unhappy if they cannot almost every instant covet joys that have never been seen before—of this I am well aware.

On the whole I consider a constant need for delight and diversion in completely new things to be a sign of pettiness, lack of inner life, of estrangement from nature, and of a mediocre or defective gift of understanding. It is little children for whom one must always be producing something new and different, in order to stop their being dissatisfied. The serious writer can in no way feel called upon to supply an accumulation of material, to act the agile servant of fretful greed; and consequently he is not at all afraid of a few repetitions, although of course he takes continual, industrious trouble to forfend frequent similarities.

It was now evening and I came to a quiet, pretty path or side road which ran under trees, toward the lake, where my walk ended.

In a forest of alders close to the water, a school for boys and girls had assembled and the parson or teacher was giving instruction in botany and the observation of nature, here in the midst of nature, at nightfall. As I walked slowly onward, two figures arose in my mind.

Perhaps because of a general weariness, or for some other reason, I thought of a beautiful girl, and of how alone in the wide world I was, which could not possibly be right.

Self-reproof touched me from behind my back and stood before me in my way. Certain evil memories took control of me. Accusations of all sorts that I directed toward myself made my heart a burden to me. I had to struggle hard.

While I searched for and picked flowers all around me, partly in the little forest, partly in the fields, it softly began to rain, whereupon the delicate countryside became even more delicate and still. As I listened to the rain rustling gently down upon the leaves, it seemed to me that tears fell. How sweet gentle, warm summer rain is!

Old, long-past failures occurred to me, disloyalty, scorn, falsity, cunning, hatred, and many unbeautiful, violent actions, wild desire, uncontrolled passion. Clearly I saw before me how I had hurt people sometimes, and done wrong. In the whispering delicate sounds all around me, my pensiveness increased till it became sorrow.

Like a packed stage of suspenseful scenes from a drama

my former life opened to me, in such a way that I was seized with astonishment at my countless frailties, unfriendliness of various sorts as well as all the lovelessness which I had caused people to feel.

Then there came before my eyes the second figure, and suddenly I saw again the old, poor, forsaken man whom I had seen lying on the ground a few days before, so pitiful, deathly and pale, lamentable, so sorrowful and weary to death that the sight of him had terrified me and choked my soul. This weary man I now saw in my mind's eye, and a feeling almost of nausea took hold of me.

Since I wished to lie down somewhere and by chance a cozy little place by the lakeside was quite nearby, I made myself as comfortable as I could, tired as I felt, on soft ground under a friendly tree's artless branches.

As I observed earth and air and sky, a melancholy overwhelming thought seized hold of me that forced me to say to myself that I was a poor prisoner between heaven and earth, that we all were miserably locked up in such a way, that for all of us there was nowhere a path into the other world save the one path that led down into the pit, into the earth, into the grave.

"So then this rich life, all beautiful, bright colors, this joy in life, and all human meaning, friendship, family, and beloved, the tender air full of gay, delightful thoughts, houses of fathers, houses of mothers, and dear gentle roads, moon and high sun, and the eyes and hearts of men must one day fade away and die."

As I asked mankind to forgive me, still lying there deep in thought, that girl fresh with youth came once more to mind with her so childish, pretty mouth and enchanting cheeks. Vividly I imagined how bewitched I was by her bodily form with its melodious sweetness, but how when I had asked her not long ago whether she believed I was sincerely devoted to her, in her doubt and disbelief her lovely eyes had looked away, and she had said No.

Circumstances had prompted her to travel, and with this she was lost to me. Yet I would probably have been able to convince her that I meant well with her. I should have told her, while there was still time, that my feelings were utterly honest. It would have been so simple and certainly only right to confess to her openly: "I love you. All your concerns are as important to me as my own. For many dear, beautiful reasons I wish to make you happy." But since I had thought no more of it, she went away.

"Did I pick flowers to lay them upon my sorrow?" I asked myself, and the flowers fell out of my hand. I had risen up, to go home, for it was late now and everything was dark.

Robert Walser

"A clairvoyant of the small."   —W. G. Sebald

"One of the profoundest products of modern literature."
   —Walter Benjamin

Robert Walser was born in Biel, Switzerland, in 1878. After leaving school at age fourteen, he worked as a copyist, clerk, inventor's assistant, and butler before settling in Berlin to become a writer. It was here that Walser would pen many of his most famous works, including *The Tanners*, *The Assistant*, and *Jakob von Gunten*. In 1913, after several years of struggling with writer's block, Walser returned to Switzerland, where he continued to publish and sought alternative means of income. By the end of the 1920s, his increasingly unstable mental health led him to seek help, and he spent the rest of his life in sanatoriums. Walser died on Christmas Day, 1956, while out for a walk.

The poet and translator **Christopher Middleton** (b. 1926) is responsible for originally bringing the work of Robert Walser to an English-language readership. He translated *Selected Stories*, *Jakob von Gunten*, and *Speaking to the Rose*.

Susan Bernofsky has translated six books by Robert Walser, including *Microscripts*, *The Tanners*, and *The Assistant*. She is currently at work on a Walser biography.